Families

For Niviaq. —Jesse Unaapik Mike

For River. —Kerry McCluskey

Published by Inhabit Media Inc. · www.inhabitmedia.com

Inhabit Media Inc. (Iqaluit), P.O. Box 11125, Iqaluit, Nunavut, X0A 1H0
(Toronto), 191 Eglinton Avenue East, Suite 301, Toronto, Ontario, M4P 1K1

Design and layout copyright © 2017 Inhabit Media Inc.
Text copyright © 2017 by Jesse Mike and Kerry McCluskey
Illustrations by Lenny Lishchenko copyright © 2017 Inhabit Media Inc.

Editors: Neil Christopher and Kelly Ward
Art director: Danny Christopher
Designer: Astrid Arijanto

We acknowledge the support of the Canada Council for the Arts for our publishing program.

This project was made possible in part by the Government of Canada.

ISBN: 978-1-77227-161-4

Library and Archives Canada Cataloguing in Publication

Mike, Jesse, author
        Families / by Jesse Mike and Kerry McCluskey ; illustrated
by Lenny Lishchenko.

ISBN 978-1-77227-161-4 (softcover)

        1. Families--Juvenile literature. I. McCluskey, Kerry, 1968-,
author II. Lishchenko, Lenny, illustrator III. Title.

HQ744.M54 2017   j306.85   C2017-906753-2

Printed in Canada

Families

By Jesse Unaapik Mike and Kerry McCluskey
Illustrated by Lenny Lishchenko

INHABIT MEDIA

"*Anaana*, where does my dad live?" Talittuq said as he sat at the table, eating his breakfast before his first day of grade two.

Anaana answered, "Your dad lives in Mittimatalik, Talittuq. And we live in Iqaluit."

"Why doesn't he live here with us? My cousin's *ataata* lives with him. Why doesn't my dad live with us?" asked Talittuq.

"Because every family is different," Anaana answered. "Some families have an anaana and an ataata living in the same house, but in our family, it's just me and you. And even though there is no ataata here, we have lots of love and happiness in our home, right?"

"Right," said Talittuq. Anaana leaned over the table and kissed Talittuq right on the nose.

Talittuq had asked his anaana this question lots and lots of times before, but he still didn't understand why his family was different from his cousin's family. He didn't want to be different. He wanted to be the same. He wanted to have a dad who took him to hockey and soccer practice and who wrestled with him.

He finished up his cereal and brushed his teeth. Talittuq kissed his anaana goodbye and rode his bike to school. He was excited about his first day of grade two. He was also excited because today was the first time his anaana had agreed to let him ride his bike to school all by himself.

When Talittuq got to school, he parked his bike at the bike rack and ran as fast as he could to the monkey bars. Over the summer, Talittuq had learned how to swing across the bars from one end to the other and he wanted to show his friends how strong he was, now that he was in grade two.

"Hey Qaukkai, watch this," yelled Talittuq to his friend Qaukkai.

As he swung his body around and around on the monkey bars, he almost knocked Qaukkai over as she watched him. Qaukkai was just starting kindergarten and she was smaller than Talittuq. She ducked to avoid Talittuq, but it startled her and she began to cry.

Talittuq sat down beside her and held her hand. "Are you okay? Do you want me to go get your anaana or your mom?" Talittuq asked.

Both of Qaukkai's parents had come to school with her on her first day of kindergarten. Talittuq ran to get them, but they were talking to another woman whom Talittuq did not know. Talittuq knew it was rude to interrupt adults when they were talking, but Qaukkai was still crying. He tugged at Qaukkai's anaana's sleeve to get her attention. "Qaukkai needs you," said Talittuq.

Qaukkai's anaana ran to her and picked her up and wiped away her tears. Qaukkai's mom said to Talittuq, "Thank you for looking out for Qaukkai, Talittuq."

"Yes, thank you," said the woman whom Talittuq didn't know.

"Talittuq, this is Qaukkai's *puukuluk*, her birth mother. We adopted Qaukkai from her," Qaukkai's mom said. Talittuq thought Qaukkai must be the luckiest girl in the whole town to have three moms.

The bell rang just then and all the kids lined up to go to their classrooms.

Talittuq's best friend, Johnny, who was also his cousin, lined up beside him. Talittuq was very happy to see Johnny because Johnny, his brothers, and his anaana and ataata had been away all summer visiting family. Talittuq had missed them terribly while they were gone.

They filed into the school and hung their backpacks on their coat hooks. They found their desks and sat down. Today was Talittuq's first day with his new teacher, Taiviti.

"Good morning, class. My name is Taiviti and I am going to be your grade two teacher this year. I just moved to Iqaluit with my family, and I am looking forward to getting settled into the school and into our new home. I live right beside the school, just over there, with my husband and my son."

Talittuq had already met Taiviti and his family at the skate park. He thought they were really cool because they were awesome

As Taiviti took attendance, Talittuq's friend Joanasie came running into the classroom. He was always late. Joanasie had also been away all summer visiting his mom in Ottawa. He lived in Iqaluit with his ataata, but his mom lived down south.

Joanasie whispered to Talittuq, "I went to hockey camp with my brothers and my stepdad in Ottawa. My anaana was busy with my new baby sister, so we went to hockey camp every day. I scored a million goals."

"You're so lucky," whispered Talittuq, wishing that he could have gone to hockey camp, too.

Soon enough, it was time to go home for lunch. Talittuq was anxious to get home to his anaana to tell her about his first morning at school. On his way out of the school, he saw Maggie, his teacher from last year. Talittuq gave her a big hug and pulled a small bag of berries out of his pocket.

"Here you go, Maggie. My anaana and I picked these just for you to share with Jane," said Talittuq. Jane was Maggie's granddaughter. She had lived with Maggie ever since her anaana had gotten sick.

"Thank you, Talittuq. We will have them for dessert at lunchtime," said Maggie.

When Talittuq got home, he ran inside. Anaana was sitting at the table with Talittuq's favourite lunch, seal ribs. He washed his hands, and as he sat down to eat, he thought about what his anaana had said before: every family is different. He realized that his anaana was right! He had friends and cousins who lived with two moms, two dads, a mom and a dad, a grandma, and a stepdad.

"Anaana, you're right!" said Talittuq. "All families are different!"

"That's right, Talittuq, and we all have love and happiness in our homes," said Anaana, and she leaned over and kissed him right on the nose.

anaana (a-naa-na)—Inuktitut word for mother

ataata (a-taa-ta)—Inuktitut word for father

Joanasie (Joe-anna-see)—An Inuktitut name

puukuluk (poo-coo-luke)—Inuktitut word for birth mother

Qaukkai (Kow-kai)—An Inuktitut name

Taiviti (Tie-vee-tee)—An Inuktitut name

Talittuq (Ta-leet-took)—An Inuktitut name

Contributors

Jesse Unaapik Mike was born and raised in Iqaluit, Nunavut, where she lives with her partner, Moriah, and her daughter, Niviaq. She is raising her daughter through shared custody and hopes to raise her daughter in a better world with more love and less hate. Jesse has been advocating for Inuit youth since she was a teenager and has built on this to advocate for all Inuit on issues that most people will not speak of.

Kerry McCluskey lived in Yellowknife, Northwest Territories, for five years before moving to Iqaluit, Nunavut, in 1998 to work as a journalist. Nearly twenty years later, Kerry continues to write and has built a wonderful home in Iqaluit with her son, River Talittuq Sukaq Gordon McCluskey. Her son features prominently in many of the stories she tells.

Lenny Lishchenko is not a boy. She is an illustrator, graphic designer, and comics maker who will never give up the chance to draw a good birch tree. Ukrainian born and Canadian raised, she's interested in telling stories that people remember years later, in the early mornings when everything is quiet and still. She's worked with clients such as Lenny Letter, Power Athletics Ltd, Alberta Venture, and Rubicon Publishing, and is based out of Mississauga.